The Magical Animal Fairies

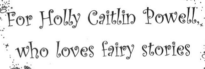

For Holly Caitlin Powell,
who loves fairy stories

to

redien

LONDON BOROUGH OF SUTTON LIBRARY SERVICE	
30119 027 075 60 7	
Askews & Holts	Jun-2013
JF	

ORCHARD BOOKS
338 Euston Road, London NW1 3BH
Orchard Books Australia
Level 17/207 Kent Street, Sydney, NSW 2000
A Paperback Original

First published in 2009 by Orchard Books.

© 2009 Rainbow Magic Limited.
A HIT Entertainment company. Rainbow Magic
is a trademark of Rainbow Magic Limited.
Reg. U.S. Pat. & Tm. Off. And other countries.
www.rainbowmagiconline.com

HiT entertainment

Illustrations © Orchard Books 2009

A CIP catalogue record for this book is available
from the British Library.

ISBN 978 1 40830 355 9
12

Printed in Great Britain

Orchard Books is a division of Hachette Children's Books,
an Hachette UK company

www.hachette.co.uk

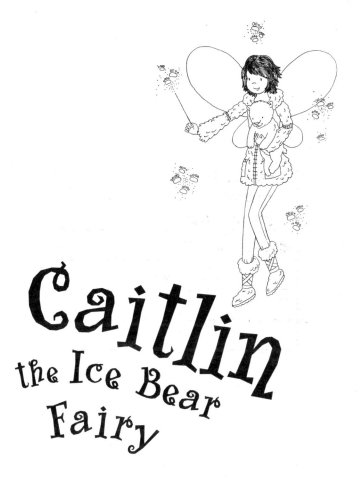

Caitlin
the Ice Bear
Fairy

by Daisy Meadows

ORCHARD

The
Fairyland
Palace

Barn

Farmhou

Stables

Clubhouse

CAMP

Adventure Lake

Birdwatching
Tower

Jack Frost's
Ice Castle

Meadows

Amphitheatre

The Labyrinth

Maze of tunnels

Cabins

Waterfall

Hills

There are seven special animals
Who live in Fairyland.
They use their magic powers
To help others where they can.

A dragon, black cat, firebird,
A seahorse and snow swan too,
A unicorn and ice bear -
I know just what to do.

I'll lock them in my castle
And never let them out.
The world will turn more miserable,
Of that, I have no doubt...

Contents

Frosty Sparkles!

"I can't believe it's the last day of our holiday already," Kirsty Tate said sadly, as she finished packing her bag and zipped it shut. She gazed around the cosy wooden cabin where she and her best friend, Rachel Walker, had spent the week with four other girls. They'd been

staying at an adventure camp and had
taken part in all sorts of activities –
exploring caves, canoeing, horseriding –
as well as making some very special
fairy friends!

The holiday was almost at an end now,
and their room-mates had packed their
bags ready to go home. Only Kirsty
and Rachel were left in the cabin.

"We've had such brilliant
adventures this week,"
Rachel said, smiling as
she thought about them.

Kirsty put on her coat.
"Well, the holiday
isn't over just yet,"
she reminded
Rachel.

"We've got High Hill to climb in a few minutes…and we've got to find the last Magical Animal, too."

Rachel nodded, an anxious expression appearing on her face. "Oh, I hope we do spot the little ice bear," she said. "I hate thinking of her being lost and alone."

"Or caught by Jack Frost's goblins," Kirsty added. "We can't let that happen."

It was rather cold outdoors, so Rachel grabbed their hats and scarves. "Come on," she said. "The sooner we get out there and start looking, the better!"

Unknown to everyone else at the holiday camp, Kirsty and Rachel had been having some extra-special adventures…helping the Magical Animal Fairies find their missing animals! Nasty Jack Frost had stolen them, but the clever animals had found a way to escape from his Ice Castle into the human world, where they'd been ever since. So far, the two girls had helped the fairies track down a baby dragon, a magic black cat, a young firebird, a seahorse, a snow swan and a unicorn.

But there was still the ice-bear cub left to find.

Rachel and Kirsty went to meet the other campers, who were gathered outside the camp clubhouse. When everyone was there, one of the counsellors, a tall man called Michael, spoke. "It's the camp tradition to climb High Hill together on the last day of our holiday," he said. "And when we get back, we're having a special goodbye party. So if everyone's ready for the hike, let's go!"

A winding path led up the tall, grassy hill and the group set off together. They hadn't gone very far before they felt a cold wind start up around them. "I'm glad I've got my gloves," Kirsty said, digging them out of her coat pockets. "It's surprisingly chilly, isn't it?"

Rachel nodded, pulling her hat a little lower over her ears. "Yes – look, there are even frost patches on the ground up ahead," she said, pointing them out.

"Oh, yes!" Kirsty said, walking faster towards them. Rachel had to jog a little to catch up with her, taking care not to slip, but Kirsty seemed to speed up even faster as she strode along the path.

Before long, the girls were quite a long way ahead of all the other campers.

Rachel glanced down and was surprised at how high they'd climbed. The camp already seemed small below them, and the staff cleaning out the cabins looked like tiny stick figures.

Rachel almost skidded on a patch of frost and quickly turned her gaze back to the path. "Maybe we should slow down," she suggested,

as Kirsty showed no signs of letting up her fast pace. "It's quite slippery here."

Kirsty shrugged. "We'll be fine," she said. "I feel like I could do anything!"

Rachel glanced at her friend in surprise. Kirsty seemed to be in an odd mood! But before Rachel could say anything, they heard Michael shout out behind them, "Girls, slow down! It's not a race! You guys are leaving the rest of us behind!"

Rachel turned to see Michael waving at them. "Find a spot to wait for the rest of the group," he called. "Let everyone catch up, OK?"

"OK," Rachel agreed, but Kirsty didn't seem to have heard.

"Rachel, look," she was saying urgently, grabbing her friend's arm. "Look at that gorse bush over there – it's covered in sparkles!"

Rachel gazed over to where Kirsty was pointing. Sure enough, the dark green bush was lit up with tiny twinkling lights. Was it more frost or was it—

Before she could finish her question, a tiny fairy fluttered out of the bush, with a trail of glittering fairy dust behind her. It was Caitlin the Ice Bear Fairy!

Too Late!

Caitlin had short brown hair and sparkly brown eyes. She was wearing a fluffy lilac coat with a furry pink collar, turquoise leggings with sparkles on them and big furry boots. "Hello, girls," she said. "I'm looking for Crystal, my ice bear. Have you seen her anywhere?"

"I'm sure we can find her," Kirsty said confidently. She put her hands on her hips. "Maybe I should climb a tree to get a proper look around?"

Rachel gave her friend a confused look. "I'm not sure that's a good idea," she said slowly.

"This bit of the hill is so steep…if you fell, you could be really hurt."

"I won't fall!" Kirsty cried airily.

Rachel stared at her. Kirsty was acting so strangely today! "Are you all right?" she asked.

Caitlin smiled. "I think I know why Kirsty is feeling so courageous," she said. "It's because of Crystal the ice bear's magic — she must be somewhere nearby!"

Rachel smiled too. Of course! At the start of their adventure, she and Kirsty had learned that each of the seven Magical Animals had a very special power — such as humour, imagination, courage and compassion.

The Magical Animal Fairies trained the animals and taught them how to use their powers, so that they could spread their gifts throughout the human world as well as Fairyland. Crystal's power was the gift of courage.

"Remember, a Magical Animal's power can become stronger or even work in the opposite way when they are nervous or scared," Caitlin reminded them. "And their powers affect people who are close to them!"

Kirsty looked excited. "So where is Crystal?" she wondered aloud. "I can't see her, but it's definitely cold enough for an ice bear around here."

Just then, Caitlin let out a gasp and pointed to a sparkling, icy trail nearby, which led further up the hill. "Look how thick that ice is," she said. "I've got a horrible feeling that Jack Frost has been here. He must be searching for Crystal, too!"

Even Kirsty felt her confidence fade
when she heard this. She and Rachel had
met cold, spiky Jack Frost several times
by now, and he was really scary. But she
hated the thought of little Crystal being
caught by him even more than she
dreaded seeing him herself. "We've got to
track them both down – and fast," she
said in a determined voice. "Maybe…"

"Sssshh," Rachel hissed, elbowing her.
The campers' voices and
laughter were much
louder now, as
Michael and the rest
of the group caught
them up. Caitlin had
to duck into the folds
of Rachel's scarf so that
she wouldn't be seen.

"We're going to have a short break," Michael announced to everyone. "It's been a tough climb and there's still some way to go before we'll reach the top. I've got a flask of hot chocolate here and snacks – come and help yourselves, then find a quiet spot to take a rest."

Kirsty raised an eyebrow at Rachel, who nodded. This sounded like the perfect opportunity to sneak up the icy trail in search of Jack Frost! They grabbed some biscuits and set off at once, clambering carefully up the frozen path.

It was very slippery and both girls had to tread carefully, clinging to the shrubs either side of the hill trail so as not to lose their footing. Jack Frost might have deliberately made the path icy to put them off finding Caitlin, Rachel thought glumly as she almost skidded for the third time. It wouldn't surprise her. He was so horrible!

Five minutes' slipping and sliding later, the girls were so far up the path, they could barely hear the sound of their friends further down the hill. The trail twisted around the corner…and then the girls stopped abruptly as they saw who was standing just metres ahead: Jack Frost! He had a little white bear cub on an icy leash and was smiling in a horribly gloating way.

"You're too late!" he cried, his voice ringing out through the cold air. "The ice bear is mine again.

Those idiot goblins – I should have known better than to entrust them with bringing back the Magical Animals. If you want a job doing properly, you've got to do it yourself. And now I have the ice bear, and it will make me the most courageous creature in Fairyland!"

Caitlin fluttered out from her hiding place, her face a picture of dismay at the sight of Crystal on a lead. The ice bear gave a growl of unhappiness as she saw her mistress, and strained to be freed. But Jack Frost merely pulled the lead tighter so that Crystal couldn't move.

"You're making a mistake," Caitlin cried, her voice shaking. "Stealing Crystal won't guarantee you courage — her magic doesn't work like that."

"Well, it's working just fine so far," Jack Frost snarled. "I feel full of courage — and very confident that you'll never get her back again!" He waved his wand and was surrounded by glittering blue icy magic. In the blink of an eye, he and Crystal had completely vanished.

To Jack Frost's Castle

"We've got to go after him," Rachel said, as the last blue sparkles from Jack Frost's magic faded into nothing. "Time will stand still here while we're in Fairyland, won't it? Let's try to find him there!"

"We must," Caitlin agreed, her face pale. "We'll go to his Ice Castle right away!" She waved her wand and a flood of sparkly lilac fairy dust swirled around the three of them, wrapping the girls in a glittering whirlwind and lifting them off their feet.

A few seconds later, they landed again and the whirlwind disappeared. Now they were in Fairyland – and Kirsty and Rachel had both been turned into fairies, with their own shimmering wings on their backs!

Kirsty shook out her wings with a smile, then looked around. They were standing in a snow-covered garden outside a tall, forbidding-looking castle with icy blue turrets. Jack Frost's castle!

"My magic won't take us inside the castle," Caitlin explained. "We'll have to sneak in somehow to see if Jack Frost is there." She fluttered her wings and rose a few metres off the ground. "Come on, let's fly around and see if we can spot a way in."

The three friends flew high into the air and began circling the castle. Down below, there were goblins running about, shouting. "There's a bear in the castle!" the fairies heard one cry fretfully.

"I saw it – and it had such sharp teeth! There's no way I'm going in there again!"

"That's interesting," Caitlin said, hovering in mid-air as she watched them. "Looks like Crystal's courage magic is working in reverse on these goblins. They seem very nervous." A hopeful expression appeared on her face. "I wonder if all this running around means they've left the castle unguarded? We might be able to get in quite easily."

The three of them fluttered around, searching for a way into the castle. But unfortunately the windows were all barred, and there were goblin guards on the turrets. There were also two goblins at the huge doors that were the main entrance to the castle. These goblins looked nervous about something, too, and the fairies flew closer so that they could listen to their conversation.

"Jack Frost is going to be really cross if he doesn't get his ice lollies soon," one of them said fearfully. "But I daren't go in the same room as that bear!" "I heard it growling a minute ago," the second goblin said, shivering. "What are we going to do?"

Rachel smiled as an idea suddenly came to her. "We could offer to take the ice lollies in!" she hissed. "Caitlin, would you be able to use your magic to make us look like goblins?"

Caitlin nodded. "Yes," she replied, her face lighting up. "Great idea — then we can get close to Jack Frost and Crystal too, hopefully. The only thing is, turning us all into goblin look-alikes will take a lot of magic, and the effects won't last for very long…"

"Then we'll just have to be as quick as we can," Kirsty said. "I think it's our only chance!"

Looking Green!

The three friends quickly found a
deserted corner of the castle grounds and
Caitlin waved her wand, muttering a
string of magical-sounding words as she
did so. There was a green flash of light
and a swirl of lilac fairy dust, and then
Rachel and Kirsty felt the strangest
sensation in their faces – as if their skin

was stretching! Kirsty reached up to pat
her face tentatively and her eyes goggled
in surprise when she felt how long and
bumpy her nose was. Oh, and her ears
felt enormous when she touched them!

She looked at the other two and burst
into giggles. They were hardly
recognisable as Rachel and Caitlin – as
they both looked just like sneaky green
goblins!

"I don't know why you're laughing,"
Rachel chuckled, elbowing her. "You're
not looking so pretty yourself!"

"We should hurry," Caitlin reminded them. "My magic won't last long, and Crystal's magic might be reversed any second, making the goblins super-confident instead of nervous."

The three of them went swiftly to the entrance of the castle, where the goblin guards were still arguing about the ice lollies.

"We'll take them," Kirsty offered, trying to make her voice deep like a goblin's. Her heart pounded as she waited for them to reply. Would the disguise fool them?

The guards exchanged a crafty look. "Sure," one said, pushing the box of ice lollies over. "It's totally safe in there. There's no bear or anything...ow!" He yelped as the other goblin trod heavily on his toe.

Rachel pressed her lips together, trying not to smile. So far, so good! "Is Jack Frost in his throne room?" she asked.

"Yep," the second guard replied. "With that scary b—" He broke off, obviously not wanting the girls and Caitlin to change their minds. "With nothing," he amended hastily.

"Fine," Kirsty said, taking the box. "Come on, guys."

Once past the guards, the three friends ran through the vast icy corridors towards Jack Frost's throne room. They'd been inside the castle many times now, and knew which way to go.

As they hurried along though, Kirsty noticed with a lurch of dread that Rachel's hands were no longer quite so green as they had been. "I think the magic might be wearing off," she said nervously. "Look at your hands, Rachel!"

Rachel stared down in dismay, then inspected Kirsty's face. "Your nose isn't as pointy as it was, either," she said. "We've got to get there as soon as possible!"

"We need to work out our plan, too," Caitlin realised. "How are we actually going to get Crystal back, once we're in the throne room?"

"It's probably best if you free Crystal, as she knows you," Rachel said, thinking fast as they rushed along. "So perhaps Kirsty and I can distract Jack Frost so that you have a chance to slip over to her?"

"I think that's a good idea," Kirsty agreed, just as they reached the throne room.

"Me too," Caitlin said, taking a deep breath. "Come on, then. Let's do it."

Kirsty rapped on the door and they walked in, trying to look as business-like as possible.

Jack Frost was sitting on his icy throne, drumming his fingers on the arm rest. Tied to the throne by an icy leash was Crystal, who was lying with her head on her paws.

"Poor thing," Caitlin murmured under her breath. "She looks so unhappy!"

The throne room was chilly and grand, lit by icy chandeliers and paved with a stone floor. Rachel could feel goosebumps prickling along her arms, and her teeth chattered with the cold. Jack Frost looked up at the new arrivals, and his eyes narrowed to slits. Rachel's heart skipped a beat. Had he recognised them?

Found Out!

Kirsty, too, was worried at the sight of Jack Frost's expression. Then she realised he was staring at the box of ice lollies. "About time!" he snarled. "What kept you?"

"Our apologies," Kirsty said, bowing respectfully.

"Well, hurry up, bring me a green lolly, then," he snapped, holding his hand out.

A thought struck Kirsty. Perhaps this was a good opportunity to distract Jack Frost! She plucked a red ice lolly from the box and took it to him, her heart pounding. "Here you are," she said.

Jack Frost glared at the red ice lolly, then at Kirsty. "Green, you fool! I said, green! This is red!"

Kirsty pretended to look surprised. "Red? It looks green to me, sir," she said in her goblin voice.

Rachel guessed what her friend was playing at. "I'd say that was green, too," she agreed.

Jack Frost snorted. "Are you colour-blind as well, then? For goodness' sake! It is *red*! And I want a *green* lolly. Goblin green, like you lot!"

Kirsty had a nervous moment when he said "goblin green". If Jack Frost looked closely at them, he would see that they were looking less green by the second. Caitlin's magic was wearing off quickly now — too quickly

for her liking! Thankfully he seemed
more bothered about his lolly than
anything else at the moment, but she
knew that could all change…

"Is *this* green?" Rachel asked innocently,
holding up a yellow lolly.

Jack Frost groaned.
"No, that's yellow," he
replied. "Don't they
teach you anything at
goblin school? Get me a
green lolly – and get it now,
before I lose my temper!"

The argument went on like this
for a few moments until Jack Frost
finally snatched the box of lollies out
of Kirsty's hand. "I've had enough – I'll
get one myself," he said, rummaging
through them.

While his head was down, Caitlin made a dash towards Crystal. She whipped her magic wand from her pocket and pointed it at Crystal's icy leash, melting it with fairy magic in an instant. Jack Frost was still so busy sorting  through the lollies, he didn't see a thing.

Caitlin smiled joyfully at the little ice bear. "Hello, Crystal!" she said…but the bear cub backed away from her suspiciously.

"She thinks you're a goblin!" Kirsty hissed to Caitlin. "You're going to have to turn us back into fairies!"

She'd tried to say the words quietly, but
Jack Frost had excellent hearing and
snapped his head up at once, his eyes
cold. "What did you just say?" he snarled
– and then a furious expression spread
over his face as he saw that Crystal had
been set free…and that Caitlin had
a fairy wand in her hand!

Kirsty and Rachel both felt frozen with
fear, but thankfully

Caitlin
moved like
lightning,
pointing
her wand
at the
girls and
then
herself.

Instantly, the three of them were all
fairies again and able to fly up into the
air away from Jack Frost, who looked as
if he might very well explode with rage!

"Come back here, you horrible fairies!"
he yelled, dropping the box of ice lollies
and reaching for his own wand.

Crystal, meanwhile, let out a happy-
sounding rumble at the sight of her fairy
mistress and started to gallop across
towards her. She stopped short at the
sound of Jack Frost's loud shout.

"I haven't finished with you yet," Jack
Frost bellowed, and swished his wand
through the air. Icy lightning bolts shot
from its tip, crackling with magic as they
hurtled towards Kirsty and Rachel.

"Look out!" screamed Rachel. "Duck!"

A Perfect Party

The lightning bolts were fast and dangerous, and Kirsty and Rachel had to dive and dodge this way and that to avoid being hit. The ice bolts crashed against the walls and smashed through the windows, shattering the glass.

Kirsty was terrified as she swerved back and forth. She knew that if she was hit by one of the lightning bolts, she wouldn't stand a chance!

But then Crystal let out a roar, showing all her sharp white teeth… and suddenly Jack Frost didn't look so confident any more. In fact, as Crystal roared again, and then growled, Jack Frost shrank away against the wall, his wand dropping out of his shaking fingers.

"He's terrified!" Rachel hissed to Kirsty. She'd never seen their old enemy look so frightened before. His lower lip was actually trembling, as if he were about to cry!

Caitlin winked at them. "Clever Crystal has used her magic — in reverse," she explained in a low voice. "Now Jack Frost has no confidence whatsoever. The magic won't last long though, so we should get away while we can. Let's go!"

Crystal ran to her mistress, changing back to fairy-size as she did so. Caitlin waved her magic wand, showering them all in a cascade of glittery fairy dust which whipped up a whirlwind around them and took them whizzing away.

They landed again outside the
Fairyland Palace, and as their feet
touched the ground, Rachel and
Kirsty saw that quite a
crowd was there to
greet them! There
was Ashley the
Dragon Fairy,
Lara the
Black Cat
Fairy, Erin
the Firebird
Fairy, Rihanna
the Seahorse
Fairy, Sophia the
Snow Swan Fairy and
Leona the Unicorn Fairy –
and they all had their Magical
Animals with them. The King and

Queen of Fairyland were there too – and all the fairies cheered as they saw that Crystal had been safely reunited with Caitlin. "You did it!" cried Ashley, and her baby dragon, Sizzle, sent a burst of flames into the air in excitement. "Well done," smiled Lara, her small black cat winding around her ankles, purring as loud as an engine.

"My dears," King Oberon said, stepping forward, and smiling. "Once again, you have helped us enormously.

We are so grateful to you for what you've done, reuniting all our Magical Animal Fairies with their charges."

"And we're so proud of your bravery and quick-thinking too," the Queen continued warmly. "Fairyland and the human world will both be better places now our fairies can train the Magical Animals!"

"We'd like to throw a special party in your honour," the King said. "It's our way of saying thank you."

Rachel beamed at these words. "That sounds wonderful," she said. "But we should be thanking you!"

"Especially since we've seen how miserable life would be without the Magical Animals' gifts," Kirsty said. "It was horrible when I lost my imagination – I'm so glad the fairies are there to train the animals and spread their lovely powers around."

The Magical Animal Fairies all
looked delighted at Kirsty's words.
And then, Kirsty and Rachel's old
friends, the Party Fairies, flew in to help
the King and Queen work some
amazing party magic! Within moments,
the palace courtyard had been decorated
with huge bunches of colourful balloons,
twinkling fairy lights and glittering
streamers. A Fairyland
band played on a
stage, with Belle the
snow swan singing
a lively melody.

Lucky the black cat was up on her hind legs, dancing with Twisty the unicorn. Giggles the firebird swooped around telling jokes and making everyone laugh, while Sizzle sent bursts of fire into the air, creating wonderful fireworks. And somehow Bubbles the seahorse had arranged a spectacular water display in the fountain!

"This is amazing," Rachel said, gazing around in wonder. "It's the best party ever!"

Kirsty agreed. The walls echoed with the sound of laughter and singing, and everyone was smiling and happy. After she and Rachel had had a wonderful time dancing with Lucky and Twisty, and eating some of the delicious fairy party food, they knew they should get back to their own world.

"Thanks again for everything," Caitlin said, flying over and hugging them each in turn.

"You were both brilliant today: truly courageous, even without Crystal's magic!"

"Thank you," Kirsty said, stroking the cub's soft white fur. "And I'm so happy we could help you rescue Crystal!"

"I've loved our adventures with you and the other Magical Animal Fairies," Rachel added, waving at their new friends with a lump in her throat. "Bye!"

After they'd said all their goodbyes,
Queen Titania threw a handful of
glittering fairy dust over the girls, and
a shimmering whirlwind picked them up
and took them back to the human world.

Kirsty and Rachel found themselves on
High Hill again…but noticed almost
immediately how much warmer it was
there now. "That's because
Jack Frost has gone,"
Kirsty said
happily, looking
around. "Oh,
isn't the view
amazing from
up here?"

Rachel agreed. There below them lay the camp surrounded by lush trees and meadows. They could see the blue lake, the winding river and the rushing waterfall, all sparkling in the sunshine. "The world looks perfect," she said, feeling very content.

Kirsty smiled. "The world *is* perfect, now that we've helped the Magical Animal Fairies find their animals!" she said.

Rachel slipped an arm through Kirsty's. "We'd better go and find Michael and the rest of the group," she said. "I guess we'll be going back for the camp party soon... Two parties in one day! We're so lucky."

"We are," Kirsty agreed. "We're the luckiest girls in the world." She smiled at Rachel, and then the two friends set off happily together.

Now it's time for Kirsty and Rachel
to help...

Nicole the Beach Fairy

Read on for a sneak peek...

"Isn't it wonderful to be back on
Rainspell Island again, Rachel?" Kirsty
Tate said happily, gazing out over the
shimmering, blue-green sea. "It hasn't
changed a bit!"

Rachel Walker, Kirsty's best friend,
nodded. "Rainspell is still as beautiful as
ever, isn't it?" she replied, as the two girls
followed the rocky path down to the
beach. "This is one of the most special
places in the whole world!"

The Tates and the Walkers were
spending the half-term holiday on

Rainspell Island. Although it was autumn, the sky was a clear blue and the sun was shining brightly, so it felt more like summer. Kirsty and Rachel couldn't wait to get to the beach and dip their toes in the sea.

"You're right, Rachel," Kirsty agreed, her eyes twinkling. "After all, this is where we first became friends!"

"And we found lots of other wonderful friends here too, didn't we?" Rachel laughed.

Kirsty and Rachel shared an amazing secret. During their first holiday on Rainspell Island, they'd met the Rainbow Fairies, after Jack Frost's wicked spell had cast them out of Fairyland. Since then the girls had got to know many of the other fairies, and the tiny, magical friends often asked for Rachel and Kirsty's help whenever Jack Frost and his naughty goblin servants were causing problems.

"This is gorgeous!" Kirsty said, as they reached the beach at last.

The flat, golden sand seemed to stretch for miles into the distance. Seagulls soared in the sky above, and Kirsty could smell the fresh, salty sea air. "Shall we explore the rock pools, Rachel?" she suggested.

But Rachel didn't reply. She was looking along the beach, her face clouded with dismay.

"Haven't you noticed the litter, Kirsty?" she asked, pointing ahead of them...

Read Nicole the Beach Fairy to find out what adventures are in store for Kirsty and Rachel!

Meet the
Magical Animal
Fairies

Seven magical animals are lost in the human
world! Help Rachel and Kirsty reunite them
with their fairy friends.

www.rainbowmagicbooks.co.uk

Meet the fairies, play games
and get sneak peeks at
the latest books!

www.rainbowmagicbooks.co.uk

There's fairy fun for everyone on
our wonderful website.
You'll find great activities, competitions, stories and
fairy profiles, and also a special newsletter.

Get 30% off all Rainbow Magic books at
www.rainbowmagicbooks.co.uk

Enter the code RAINBOW at the checkout.
Offer ends 31 December 2013.

Offer valid in United Kingdom and Republic of Ireland only.

Win Rainbow Magic Goodies!

There are lots of Rainbow Magic fairies, and we want to know which one is your favourite! Send us a picture of her and tell us in thirty words why she is your favourite and why you like Rainbow Magic books. Each month we will put the entries into a draw and select one winner to receive a Rainbow Magic Sparkly T-shirt and Goody Bag!

Send your entry on a postcard to Rainbow Magic Competition, Orchard Books, 338 Euston Road, London NW1 3BH. Australian readers should email: childrens.books@hachette.com.au New Zealand readers should write to Rainbow Magic Competition, 4 Whetu Place, Mairangi Bay, Auckland NZ. Don't forget to include your name and address. Only one entry per child.

Good luck!

Meet the
Green Fairies

Jack Frost's goblins make a mess everywhere they go. Can Kirsty and Rachel clean things up before the natural world is seriously harmed?

www.rainbowmagicbooks.co.uk